29.00

MONKEY WITH A TOOL BELT BLASTS OFF

Chris Monroe

CAROLRHODA BOOKS MINNEAPOLIS

For Selah

Carolrhoda Books®
An imprint of Lerner Publishing Group, Inc.
241 First Avenue North
Minneapolis, MN 55401 USA

For reading levels and more information, look up this title at www.lernerbooks.com.

Designed by Danielle Carnito.
Main body text set in Blockhead OT Unplugged. Typeface provided by Emigre, Inc.
The illustrations in this book were created in pencil on illustration board and then painted in gouache and inked.

Library of Congress Cataloging-in-Publication Data

Names: Monroe, Chris, author, illustrator.
Title: Monkey with a tool belt blasts off! / Chris Monroe.
Description: Minneapolis : Carolrhoda Books, [2020] | Audience: Ages 4–8. | Audience: Grades 2–3. | Summary: Chico Bon Bon and Clark the elephant fly the Banana 5 to the Superstar Space Station to fix the snack bar's Moon Malt machine, but find a situation stickier than they anticipated.
Identifiers: LCCN 2019049739 (print) | LCCN 2019049740 (ebook) | ISBN 9781541577572 (library binding) | ISBN 9781541599390 (ebook)
Subjects: CYAC: Repairing—Fiction. | Space stations—Fiction. | Extraterrestrial beings—Fiction. | Monkeys—Fiction. | Animals—Fiction. | Mystery and detective stories.
Classification: LCC PZ7.M760 Mph 2020 (print) | LCC PZ7.M760 (ebook) | DDC [E]—dc23

LC record available at https://lccn.loc.gov/2019049739
LC ebook record available at https://lccn.loc.gov/2019049740

Manufactured in the United States of America
-46780-47771-1/16/2020

3 . . . 2 . . . 1 . . . BLAST OFF!

Chico Bon Bon was on his way to outer space!

Chico and his trusty copilot, Clark, were flying the *Banana 5* to the Superstar Space Station and Snack Bar.

The snack bar's Moon Malt machine had stopped working, and Chico Bon Bon was the best Moon-Malt-machine-fixer in the galaxy.

Chico's tool belt had all the tools a monkey would ever need in outer space.

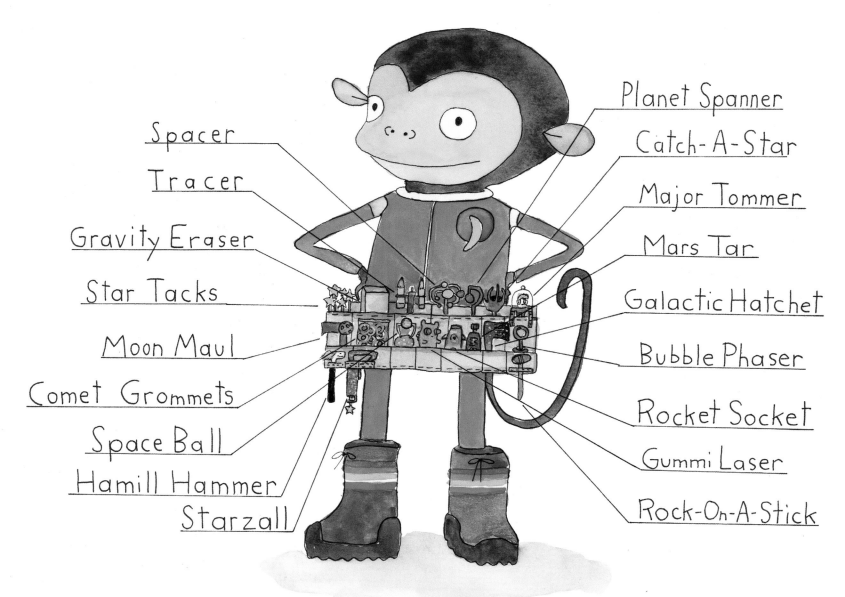

Spacer

Tracer

Gravity Eraser

Star Tacks

Moon Maul

Comet Grommets

Space Ball

Hamill Hammer

Starzall

Planet Spanner

Catch-A-Star

Major Tommer

Mars Tar

Galactic Hatchet

Bubble Phaser

Rocket Socket

Gummi Laser

Rock-On-A-Stick

"Are we there yet?" asked Clark.

Soon they could see the
space station up ahead.

They flew the *Banana 5* into the entry dock. Captain Three McGee was there to greet them. "Thank goodness you're here," she said.

We can barely function without our Moon Malt machine!

Chico got right to work . . .

Aye Aye, Captain!

He removed the back side of the Moon Malt machine.

The parts were not rusty; it looked really clean.

He checked it for problems and found not a fault,

but he pressed on the lever and still got NO MALT!

So he fixed other things that needed repair:

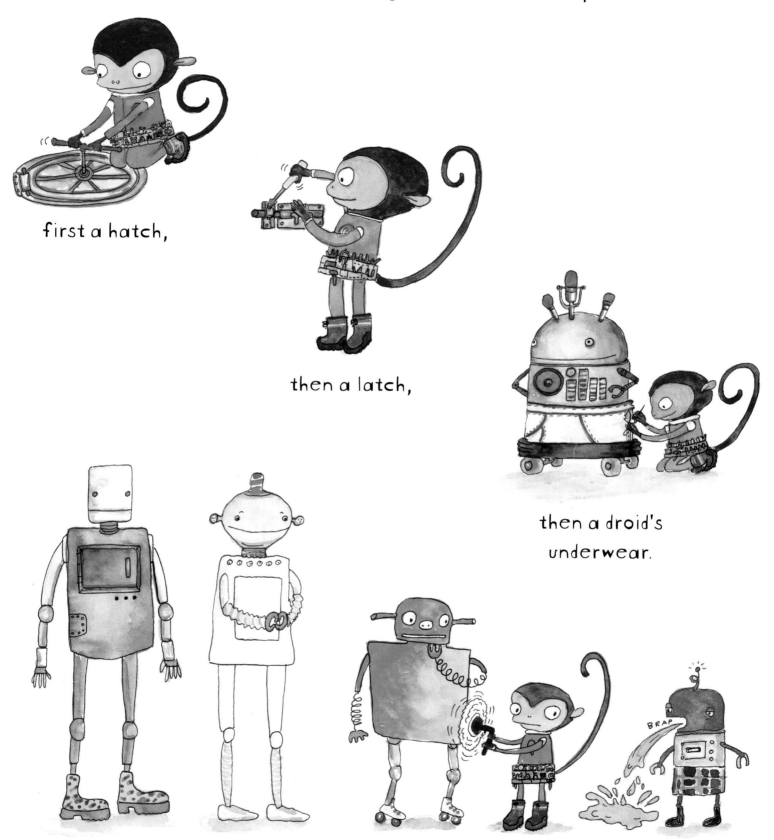

first a hatch,

then a latch,

then a droid's underwear.

He repaired several robots and cleaned them up too—
one of the robots had burped goopy goo!

Chico went back and looked inside the Moon Malt machine again. He removed another part.

What could possibly be wrong?

Something **flew** out of the machine and out the door!!

Chico did not know **WHAT** that was.

They climbed down a level and looked around.

There it was again!

FWOOSH

They followed it down the hall and it came back at them.

They climbed down another level into the break room and looked around.

Chico pulled a net out of his tool belt
and jumped high into the air.

"**What is it?**" yelled Clark, as a helpful robot pulled him out of the recycling bin.

Up close, they could see it wasn't a pom-pom.
It was a teeny tiny fuzzy creature.

The alien looked scared.

Chico took the little creature gently out of the net.

Don't worry. We won't hurt you. We're your friends.

What's your name?

"I do!" squeaked a voice from the lunch table.

It was this guy:

The captain and her crew ran in.

The droid had the tiny alien talk into a microphone on its head.

Chico had a plan.

① They took The Banana 5 to find Zootie's ship.

② Chico used his planet-matic and soon found the uncharted planet.

③ They headed that way. There it was!

④ They soon found her broken-down ship.

⑤ Chico inspected it with his no-go detector.

⑥ He saw that the battery connectors were BROKEN.

⑦ He didn't have the right parts to fix it, so he took a banana break to think about it.

⑧ He had an idea. He rummaged through Clark's lunchbox. He made a new connector with: A peanut can, A cookie box, six gummi worms

⑨ It was a little too short, so Chico made it longer with his banana peel and a tail scrunchie.

It started!

Clark gave Zootie a hug and the rest of his snacks.

They waved goodbye as Zootie headed
out into the galaxy and took a right.

Everyone piled into the *Banana 5* and headed back.

They were quiet, thinking about their new friend and hoping they would see her again someday soon.

Then Chico broke the silence:

And that's exactly what they did.

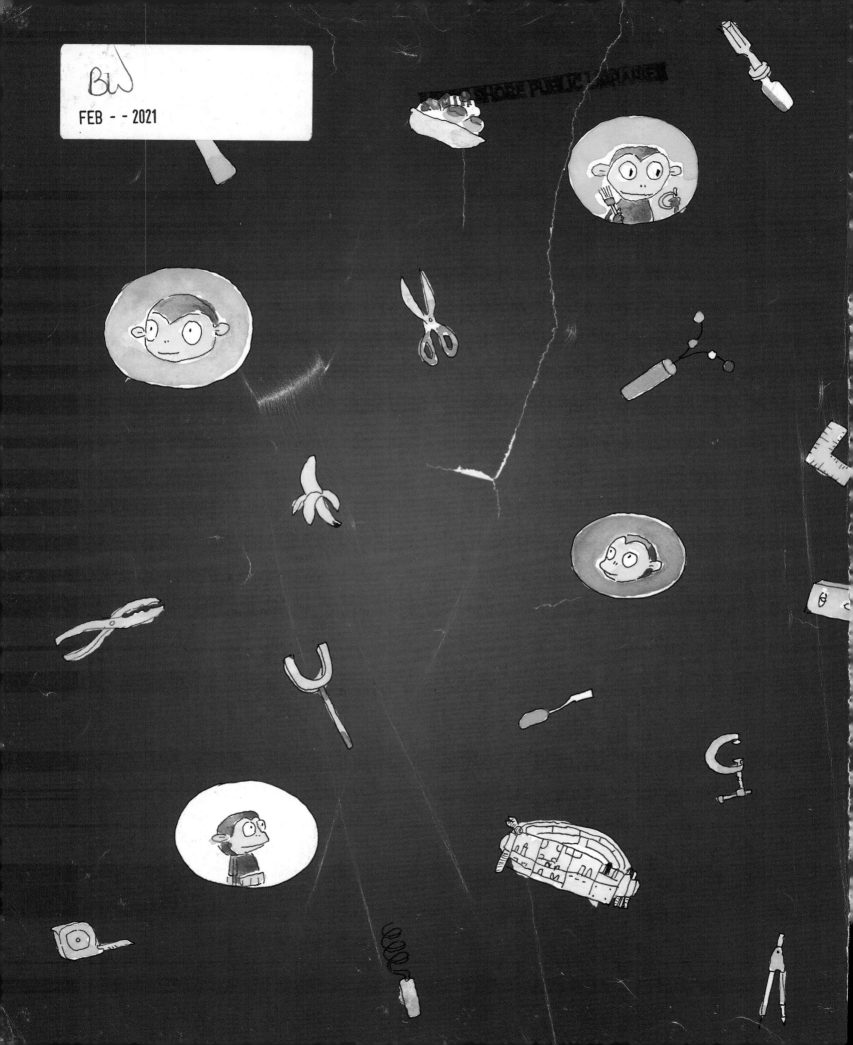